A
DOG'S
BREAKFAST

Other books in the Nightmare Club series

Help! My Brother's a Zombie!
Guinea Pig Killer
Mirrored

A DOG'S BREAKFAST

BY
ANNIE GRAVES

Little Island

A DOG'S BREAKFAST
Published 2011
by Little Island
128 Lower Baggot Street
Dublin 2
Ireland

www.littleisland.ie

ISBN 978-1-908195-16-6

Book design by Someday

Printed in Poland by Drukarnia Skleniarz

Little Island received financial assistance from
The Arts Council (An Chomhairle Ealaíon), Dublin, Ireland.

10 9 8 7 6 5 4 3 2 1

For Hugh Shalby Nameless,
a kitten with attitude

Annie Graves is twelve years old, and she has no intention of ever growing up. She is, conveniently, an orphan, and lives at an undisclosed address in the Glasnevin area of Dublin with her pet toad, Much Misunderstood, and a small black kitten, Hugh Shalby Nameless. You needn't think she goes to school — pah! — or has anything as dull as brothers and sisters or hobbies, but let's just say she keeps a large cauldron on the stove.

This is not her first book. She has written four, so far, none of which is her first.

Publisher's note: We did try to take a picture of Annie, but her face just kept fading away. We have sent our camera for investigation, but suspect the worst.

THANK YOU!

I have to give a big thanks to Katherine Farmar, because if I don't she'll send a fire-breathing demonic alien after me!

Annie here, from Glasnevin. I'm the author. That's a posh word for writer, in case you don't know. I'm not posh, but I do like posh words.

As well as being the author, I am the hostess. Which means it's my house where we have the Hallowe'en sleepover every year. A gang of us all get together, girls in the big four-poster bed, boys in sleeping bags on the floor, and we scare each other to BITS. No costumes, no torches, no special effects.

Just really scary stories.

I have this great scary story. Being an author and all, I'm good at stories. For years now, I've been trying to tell it. It's about these witches with purple skin and webbed feet and melty eyes. They fly all over the world on Hallowe'en looking for small children to kidnap and roast slowly over a fire.

But every year they all say that I'm the host, so I have to let the others tell their stories first. (Who made up that rule? I bet it was an adult.)

But at least I get to write them all down. Because I'm the best at that part. I am the Absolute Pinnacle, the Bee's Knees, the Dog's Waistcoat, the Cat's Whatever ...

OK, right, the story.

This is one that Nicola told. As a special treat, she said. Nicola's Treat is a really stupid name for a story, though. So I am calling it A Dog's Breakfast.

It could also be called a shaggy dog story.

There used to be a boy in our class named Glen. I sat next to him. Not by choice.

He disappeared, Glen. The only one who knew what had happened to him was a dog. A dog I am rather fond of, as it happens.

I never liked Glen. The rest of the O'Gearys were OK, but he sucked the fun out of everything.

Actually, I hated him. He had a high, screechy voice like a burglar alarm. I hated that burglar-alarm voice.

And I hated his lies and his complaints.
He never opened his mouth except to
complain or to lie.

When he walked to school, he
complained there was too much traffic.

When the teacher asked for his homework, he lied about why he hadn't done it.

When anyone in school asked for a loan of a pencil, he complained about having to give up one of his spares.

My mother told me that he used to lie to his mum too. (Not a good idea. They talk to each other, mums.)

When his mother went to say good night to him, when he was tucked up in bed, she would ask if he'd brushed his teeth, and he'd lie and say that he had. She knew he hadn't, but if she said so, he complained about the taste of the toothpaste.

He kept a special packet of mints under his pillow so he could breathe minty breath in her face.

She found them after he disappeared.

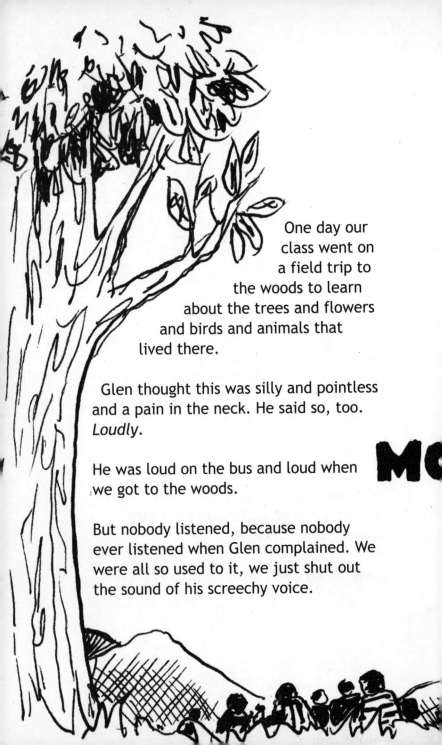

One day our
class went on
a field trip to
the woods to learn
about the trees and flowers
and birds and animals that
lived there.

Glen thought this was silly and pointless
and a pain in the neck. He said so, too.
Loudly.

He was loud on the bus and loud when
we got to the woods.

But nobody listened, because nobody
ever listened when Glen complained. We
were all so used to it, we just shut out
the sound of his screechy voice.

That made him cross, though, and he dragged his feet while the rest of us went on ahead, hiking through the woods.

MOAN

Our teacher had put us into pairs on the bus. That way, everyone in the class had someone to look out for them in case they got lost in the woods.

And wouldn't you know it, Glen was *my* partner.

That meant I was supposed to look out for him. But I didn't.

I feel a little bit bad about that now, but if I'd hung back with him, he'd only have complained about it later.

It must have taken him a while to realise he was way behind. He was probably too busy complaining to himself that the whole idea of a woodland walk was stupid.

Anyway, he wandered off the path. When you're in a wood you don't know, it's very easy to get lost if you don't pay attention. Glen wasn't good at paying attention because he was always too busy muttering to himself.

I can just imagine him now, looking around, seeing nobody and snorting. (He loved to snort.)

'Typical!' he would say, out loud. (When he wasn't muttering to himself, he was screeching, and in a wood on his own, I'd say he screeched away good-oh.) 'Now I have to find my way back to the others. And *of course* there are no signs.'

That must have been when he heard the
voice: 'I can help you with that.'

That would have made him jump,
all right! The voice had come from
nowhere, you see, or nowhere obvious,
if you get my drift. And it definitely
didn't sound like anyone Glen knew.

It wasn't anyone in his class, or any of
the teachers.

That might have been a bit scary for him, I suppose. And he didn't like being afraid, Glen.

He'd have to turn the afraid feeling into something he liked better.

'Don't do that! Don't sneak up on me like that!' he said.

He turned
around. His eyes
were rolling in his
head, trying to find
the person with the
voice.

'Higher,' said the voice, amused.

Glen looked up and saw a small person in
the branches of a tree. He couldn't tell
if the person was male or female. It was
shaped like a human but it was small.
Not small like a child. Small like a fairy.

You're wondering how I know this, aren't you? Believe me, I have my sources.

But Glen didn't believe in fairies. 'Oh, *great*,' he said. 'Is this somebody's idea of a joke? It's not funny.'

'I am not joking,' said the person. 'I can lead you back to your friends if you like. I know this wood like the back of my hand.'

'It's a stupid wood,' said Glen.

The person stared at him, blinking rapidly. Its eyes were more like a cat's eyes than a human's. 'That's not very nice,' it said. 'This wood is my home and you have insulted it.'

'Don't be stupid,' said Glen,
'nobody lives here.'

'*I* live here,' said the
small person.

Glen rolled his eyes.
'Yeah, right,' he said.
'Up that tree, I suppose.'

'Sometimes,' said the small person,
nodding. 'You are not a very nice boy.'

'I don't care what you say. You're not real. You're just a special effect. This is a waste of time.'

Glen turned around and walked in the opposite direction from the tree the person was sitting in.

But after a few steps there was the little person again, perched in a different tree. 'You won't find them on your own, you know,' the person said.

'I'm not looking for them,' said Glen.
That was a lie.

'You should be,' said the person.

'Why? I don't like them. They're all
boring.'

The small person tilted its head to one
side. 'It is easy for someone with no
imagination to be bored,' it said.

'Yeah, well ... you're annoying.' He stomped past the tree the person was sitting in.

There was a *crunch* beneath his feet. At first he probably thought it was dead leaves, but it was spring and there were no dead leaves on the ground. He lifted his foot and there was a dead snail squashed on the sole of his shoe.

'Yeurch,' he muttered, scraping his shoe against a tree trunk. 'Stupid snails.'

A moment later, he nearly tripped on the small person, who had reappeared on the path in front of him, standing squarely on the ground with its hands on its hips.

'It's not the snail's fault that you refuse to look where you're going,' it said. It was scowling now.

'If it doesn't want to get stepped on, it shouldn't live on the ground,' said Glen, as if he thought that should settle it. He made as if to step over the person, but when he tried to lift his leg he found he couldn't move.

24

'If you don't stop being such a sourpuss,
I'll do something you won't like.'

'I don't like anything you do, so that
won't be hard,' said Glen.

'Very well!' said the small person. It
waved its hands in the air and pointed
both its forefingers at Glen.

'The next time you set out to make another person feel bad, you'll start to turn into ... hmm ... something more *useful* than what you are now. If you can let a whole day pass without making anyone feel bad, you'll turn back into your old self.'

It snapped its fingers and was gone.

Glen looked around, up and down the path and in the branches of the trees, but he could see nothing. He grumbled to himself and stomped down the path.

He stepped on as many snails and worms and ladybirds as he could manage.

The wood was quite small, so it didn't take him long to find the class. We were making drawings of leaves. He found me bent over a pile of young green leaves and pinched my arm.

'OW! What are you doing?'

'I got lost because of you. You're my partner. You're supposed to watch out for me and you didn't!'

'I'm sorry,' I said, and I meant it. 'Here, I kept some paper and a pencil for you. We have to draw three different kinds of leaves.'

Glen snatched the paper and pencil from my hand. I frowned and opened my mouth as if to speak, then stopped and sniffed the air. 'Do you smell something?' I said.

'Yeah, mud and cowpats. This place is
filthy.'

'No, not that ...' I sniffed the air again.
'More like meat. It's stronger now.
Did you bring a sandwich?'

'Of course I did! Everyone had to.'

I glared at him, then shrugged. 'Must be that, then,' I said. I didn't mention that Glen's face seemed a little, well, more *pink* than it had been before.

Now,
here's the
thing. When
Glen went into
the bathroom to
wash his face the next morning,
he didn't recognise himself in the mirror.
I know this because I know what he was
turning into. His skin must have been
bright pink and glistening as if it was
coated with grease.

He would have been getting the smell,
too, by then. The smell I'd started to get
the day before.

Meat. Ham, to be more precise.

Very useful thing, ham, especially if you're hungry. Much more useful than Glen, though he probably didn't think that.

If he poked his cheek with his fingers, he'd have found that his skin was damp and soft, squidgy in a way it had never been before.

'This is *ridiculous*,' he must have said. I can just hear him saying that. Then the look on his face when he remembered he wasn't supposed to say or do anything nasty. Not if he wanted to stop turning into something ... *useful*.

But surely that didn't count. Did it? If he was the only one in the room, it couldn't possibly count. That wouldn't be fair at all!

Later that morning,
when he sat down in
his usual place at school,
I'd spread some papers over his part of
the table we shared.

I rushed to gather them up before he
started complaining but instead of his
usual moan, he said, 'Please, may I move
this stuff out of the way?'

I stared at him, my mouth wide open. 'Are you all right?' I said. 'You look feverish.'

Glen wanted to say, 'Don't ask stupid questions!' I could see it in his face.

But instead he just clenched his fists under the table and said, 'No, I'm fine. Thank you for asking.'

I blinked. 'All right, then,' I said, and moved the papers out of Glen's way.

The rest of the day was just like that. Every few minutes, Glen had a chance to say something mean or hurtful or rude, and every time I could see him keeping his words to himself.

It got harder and harder as the day wore on, until he could only keep his mouth shut by biting his lip and sucking in his cheeks. I watched him doing it. It was weird.

I followed him on the way home.

He went stomping down the street,
kicking the paving stones as he went. I'd
say he was imagining that each one was
a person he had been nice to that day.

'Only one day,' he muttered to himself. He stared at his hands. They were as pink and soft and damp as they had been in the morning.

But no pinker, no softer, no damper. At least he hadn't got any worse.

He was lumbering now, as if his body felt heavy and stiff, as if his insides were glued together.

As he turned the last corner before his own street, he caught sight of a scruffy, skinny brown dog, a lanky wolfhound he had seen around before.

This, my friends, was the person – I mean, the dog – who told me the story. You may laugh, but I'm telling you, this is what happened.

43

The dog didn't belong to anyone, as far as Glen could see. It had no collar and he had never seen it being walked. Walked, hah! This wasn't that kind of dog, for sure.

Glen came to a stop. The dog sniffed the air and whined softly, starting to drool. It felt hungry.

Now, Glen had bitten his lip and gritted his teeth all day instead of saying the things he was thinking. Even through the stuck-together feeling in his insides, he must have felt all of that meanness building up inside him like lava in a volcano.

He walked towards the dog. The dog barked and licked its chops. Its tongue was long and floppy and its teeth were sharp. With a grin and a whoop, Glen stretched his leg out to kick.

Before his foot could connect, though, a voice in the air said, 'Didn't think a dog would count, eh? Tch, tch, you are a *nasty* little boy.'

Nobody ever saw Glen again.

And as for the dog – well, next time I saw it, it looked sleek and fat and a teensy bit smug.

And you know, a funny thing. My family has a wolfhound now. Bluebell. What a coincidence!

Dogs can't talk, you say. Huh! How *else* would I know all this?

THE END

Told you it was a
shaggy dog story.
That dog, it
gives me the
collywobbles. I can
still see it licking its
greasy chops.

And it is true about the
wolfhound. Nicola's family
does have one of those, all
right, but I never heard a *word* out of it.

AAAAGHHH!

Dublin UNESCO City of Literature

NIGHTMARE CLUB DUBLIN PLACE NAMES COMPETITION

Hey there, all you dead smart readers of my deadly books!

My demon publishers tell me I have to explain this competition thingy to you. So that you can go on their miserable website

www.littleisland.ie

and enter their crumby competition and WIN some gloomy prize or other. A Meeting with Cake, I believe, in their stupid publishing house. (In Glasnevin, we call that a party, but these southsiders have to call it a Meeting with Cake.) But hey, cake is always good, even if you do have to meet a few crumbly publishers and a few dotty writers to get it, so here goes.

Listen up, now, if you like cake and can read …

Right, so there are twelve clues in total, hidden inside my four wonderful Nightmare Club books, and what you are looking for are Dublin place names. So, for example, there might be (there isn't but there might be, it's just an example) … there might be a character called O'Connell. And you would say, 'Hey, O'Connell Street, that's a place in Dublin.'

That is how you solve the clues. Easy peasy lemon squeezy. Only they are not as OBVIOUS as O'Connell Street, obviously.

So then when you have solved all the clues, you merry sleuths, you log on to www.littleisland.ie and you go to the page called Nightmare Club Competition and you get this form thingy and you write in the answers. That's how you get the cake. Or at least, that's how you get invited to the Meeting with Cake (or party, if you are from Glasnevin).

Twelve unlucky winners will be invited to the cake thingy, and one of the twelve, the unluckiest of all, will also win a book token for a million pounds. (Hah! There aren't any pounds any more, that was a joke.) I mean, a whole lot of euro. (But not a million. Come on, they are little tiny publishers, not international bankers.)

OK, so watch out for the street names and place names, all in Dublin, as you read the story, and write them down. And then get the next book and do the same. And the next, and the next. They are all called The Nightmare Club (books 1 to 4) and I wrote them. That's how you know which ones to get – clever, eh? Dead clever.

Your friend,
Annie Graves

PS: Not everyone who gets all twelve right can have the cake thingy; there isn't enough room and there isn't enough cake, so if more than twelve of yous get it right, there will have to be a raffle. OK?

PPS: The last day for entering the competition is The Last Day. Of 2011. Easy date to remember: the last day is the last day.

If you are reading this AFTER the last day of 2011, you'll have to check out the website to see if there is another competition you can enter.